TALES FOR VERY PICKY EATERS

Josh Schneider

HOUGHTON MIFFLIN HARCOURT
Boston • New York

For information about permission to reproduce selections from this book, write
to trade.permissions@hmhco.com or to Permissions, Houghton Mifflin Harcourt
Publishing Company, 3 Park Avenue, 19th Floor, New York, New York 10016.

www.hmhco.com

The text of this book is set in 13.5-point Impressum.
The illustrations were executed in watercolor, pen and ink, and colored pencil.

The Library of Congress has cataloged the hardcover edition as follows:
Schneider, Josh, 1980–
Tales for very picky eaters/by Josh Schneider
p. cm.
Summary: A father tells outlandish stories while trying to get his young son, who is a very picky
eater, to eat foods he thinks he will not like.
[1. Food habits—Fiction. 2. Fathers and sons—Fiction.] I. Title.
PZ7.S36355Tal 2011
[Fic]—dc22 2101024767

ISBN: 978-0-547-14956-1 hardcover
ISBN: 978-0-544-33914-9 paperback

Manufactured in China
SCP 18 17 16 15 14 13 12 11 10

4500768012

To Dana,
for letting me do the cooking

CONTENTS

The Tale of the
Disgusting Broccoli

"I can't eat broccoli," said James. "It's disgusting."

"Maybe there's something else you can eat," suggested James's father.

"What else is there?" asked James.

"Well, we have dirt. We have the finest dirt available at this time of the year, imported from the best dirt ranches in the country.

"This dirt has been walked on by the most skilled chefs wearing the finest French boots.

"It has been mixed by specially trained earthworms, and it is served on your very own floor."

"Ugh," said James. "What else do we have?"

"We have this fine gum, carefully chewed one thousand times by special children with very clean teeth.

"They must brush their teeth with three different brushes before they may chew this gum one thousand times especially for you.

"Or we have this very sweaty sock, soaked in sweat sweated by the world's fastest and tastiest runner, who was fed nothing but apples and cinnamon for three months before running a marathon in this very sock."

START

"Isn't there anything else to eat?" asked James.

"Well, there's this broccoli . . ."

"I'll have that," said James.

The Tale of the
Smelly Lasagna

"It's time for dinner."

"What are we having?" asked James.

"Mushroom lasagna."

"I can't eat this," said James. "It smells funny."

"Oh, dear," said James's father.

"What?" asked James.

"Nothing," said James's father. "I'll just have to fire the troll."

"What troll?"

CLANK

CLANK

"The troll living in the basement. We hired him specially to make this mushroom lasagna. He works very hard. He works all night long perfecting his recipe. Sometimes, if you lie very still in your bed, you can hear him moving around in the basement, clanking his pots and pans while he makes this mushroom lasagna for you.

CLANK

CLANK

"But if you don't like it, I suppose we will just have to tell him to leave. He'll be so upset. He'll have to go back to his old job."

"What was his old job?" asked James.

"He worked at the rat circus."

"That doesn't sound so good," said James.

"It isn't so good. It's so bad. The rats have sharp teeth and they love to bite. They will bite anything, but they especially love to bite trolls. And they eat his lunch when he isn't looking."

"Oh my gosh," said James. "Well, maybe I can just *try* it."

"That is very kind of you," said James's father. "He'll be so grateful."

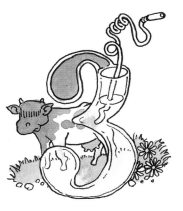

The Tale of the
Repulsive Milk

"Would you like some milk?" asked James's father.

"Blech," said James. "Milk is repulsive and I won't drink it."

"That's probably a good idea," said James's father. "Milk gives growing children strong, hard bones. Think of all the great things you could do with nice *soft* bones.

"You could scrunch yourself up into
very small places.

"You would always win at hide-and-seek.

"You could amaze your friends with amazing tricks."

CLAP
CLAP
CLAP
CLAP

"That sounds good," said James.

"Although there could be *some* problems . . . " said James's father.

"You couldn't play kickball, that's for sure.
You need strong legs to kick."

"But all my friends play kickball," said James.

"And you couldn't play baseball anymore,
either. You need strong arms to swing the
bat and throw the ball."

"But all my friends play baseball!"

"You will just have to make new friends,
I suppose.

"Or you could stay at home all day.
At least you could still scratch the dog."

"But you need strong, bony fingers to
scratch!" said James.

"Why, you're right," said James's father.
"I had forgotten."

"I guess I'd better have some milk," said James with a sigh.

"Well, if that's what you want . . ." said James's father, and he poured James a glass of milk.

The Tale of the
Lumpy Oatmeal

"I can't eat oatmeal," said James. "It's lumpy."

"Okay," said James's father.

"Okay?" asked James.

"Okay," James's father said again. "We just need to be extra careful from now on."

"Why?" asked James.

"Well, I got a great deal at the store. They were selling Growing Oatmeal. You can eat a bowl of oatmeal for breakfast and it will grow right back overnight, just in time for breakfast again. We'll never run out. It will just keep growing and growing."

"Wow," said James.

"But if we stop eating oatmeal, it will still grow a bowl a day. Before you know it, the oatmeal will outgrow the bowl."

"Really?" James asked.

"And growing oatmeal has quite an appetite. It will start eating the other foods. It will eat the leftover cake."

"But I love cake!" said James. He looked at the lumps again. "That's all right."

"And it will certainly eat the ice cream."

"But I love ice cream!" wailed James. He prodded the lumps with his spoon. "Oh, well."

"And we will have to keep a close eye on the dog, because Growing Oatmeal is not a very picky eater."

"Could you make some oatmeal with fewer lumps?" James asked.

"Why, certainly," said James's father.

The Tale of the
Slimy Eggs

"Eggs are slimy," James announced, "and I will not eat them."

"Are you sure?" asked James's father.

"Yes," said James.

"You really should try them," said James's father. "If—"

"Let me guess," interrupted James.

"If I don't eat my eggs, they'll pile up and pile up and then all the eggs will hatch and there will be chicken overload."

"No," said James's father. "No chicken overload."

"Well, then, maybe they aren't chicken eggs at all. Maybe they're dinosaur eggs, and if I don't eat my eggs, there will be Tyrannosaurus rexes and triceratopses running all over the place."

"No," said James's father. "No triceratopses."

"Okay. Then maybe you'll have to fire the troll, because one of his jobs is to break the eggs. And if I stop eating my eggs, there won't be any eggs for him to break and you'll send him back to the rat circus."

"No," said James's father. "That's not it, either."

"Then why should I try them?"

"I was just going to say that you might like them if you tried them," said James's father.

"Oh," said James.

"Okay."